"1601"

A fireside conversation with Ye Queene Eliza-beth, Shaxpur, Sr. Walter Ralegh, Ben Jonson, Lord Bacon, Francis Beaumonte, the Duchess of Bilgewater, Lady Helen, and maides of honor, from the diary of Ye Queene's cup-bearer, the Mark Twain of that day.

MARK TWAIN'S

[Date, 1601.]

Conversation
As it was by the Social Fireside
in the Time of the Tudors

Embellished

With an Illuminating Introduction,
Facetious Footnotes and a Bibliography
by FRANKLIN J. MEINE

Privately Printed for

LYLE STUART • NEW YORK

Queries regarding rights and permissions
should be addressed to
Lyle Stuart
at 225 Lafayette Street, N. Y. 12, N. Y.

Published by Lyle Stuart

Manufactured in the United States of America

To

Walter Blair, George Hiram Brownell, Bernard DeVoto,
Robert S. Forsythe, Vincent Starrett, Karl Yost
my sincere appreciation for their generous assistance.

FRANKLIN J. MEINE

"To the unconsciously indelicate all things are delicate."
"For it is not the word that is the sin, it is the spirit
  back of the word."

MARK TWAIN

CONTENTS

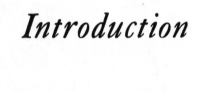

Introduction

"Born irreverent," scrawled Mark Twain on a scratch pad, "—like all other people I have ever known or heard of—I am hoping to remain so while there are any reverent irreverences left to make fun of."†

Mark Twain was just as irreverent as he dared be, and *1601* reveals his richest expression of sovereign contempt for overstuffed language, genteel literature, and conventional idiocies. Later, when a magazine editor apostrophized, "O that we had a Rabelais!" Mark impishly—and anonymously—submitted *1601;* and that same editor, a praiser of Rabelais, scathingly abused it and the sender. In this episode, as in many others, Mark Twain, the "bad boy" of American literature, revealed his huge delight in blasting the shams of contemporary hypocrisy. Too, there was always the spirit of Tom Sawyer deviltry in Mark's make-up that prompted him, as he himself boasted, to see how much holy indignation he could stir up in the world.

Who wrote 1601?

The correct and complete title of *1601,* as first issued, was: [*Date, 1601.*] *Conversation, as it was by the Social Fireside, in the Time of the Tudors.* For many years after its anonymous first issue in 1880, its authorship was variously conjectured and widely disputed. In Boston, William T. Ball, one of the leading theatrical critics during the late 90's, asserted that it was originally written by an English actor (name not divulged) who gave it to him. Ball's original, it was said, looked like a newspaper strip in the way it was printed, and may indeed have been a proof pulled in some newspaper office. In St. Louis, William Marion Reedy, editor of the St. Louis *Mirror,* had seen this famous *tour de force* circulated in the early 80's in galley-proof form; he first learned from Eugene Field that it was from the pen of Mark Twain.

---

†*Holograph manuscript of Samuel L. Clemens, in the collection of the writer.*

"Many people," said Reedy, "thought the thing was done by Field and attributed, as a joke, to Mark Twain. Field had a perfect genius for that sort of thing, as many extant specimens attest, and for that sort of practical joke; but to my thinking the humor of the piece is too mellow—not hard and bright and bitter—to be Eugene Field's." Reedy's opinion hits off the fundamental difference between these two great humorists; one half suspects that Reedy was thinking of Field's *French Crisis*.

But Twain first claimed his bantling from the fog of anonymity in 1906, in a letter addressed to Mr. Charles Orr, librarian of Case Library, Cleveland. Said Clemens, in the course of his letter, dated July 30, 1906, from Dublin, New Hampshire:

"The title of the piece is *1601*. The piece is a supposititious conversation which takes place in Queen Elizabeth's closet in that year, between the Queen, Ben Jonson, Beaumont, Sir Walter Raleigh, the Duchess of Bilgewater, and one or two others, and is not, as John Hay mistakenly supposes, a serious effort to bring back our literature and philosophy to the sober and chaste Elizabeth's time; if there is a decent word findable in it, it is because I overlooked it. I hasten to assure you that it is *not* printed in my published writings."

Twitting the Rev. Joseph Twichell

The circumstances of how *1601* came to be written have since been officially revealed by Albert Bigelow Paine in *Mark Twain, A Bibliography* (1912), and in the publication of *Mark Twain's Notebook* (1935).

1601 was written during the summer of 1876 when the Clemens family had retreated to Quarry Farm in Elmira County, New York. Here Mrs. Clemens enjoyed relief from social obligations, the children romped over the countryside, and Mark retired to his octagonal study, which, perched high on the hill, looked out upon the valley below. It was in the famous summer of 1876, too, that Mark was putting the finishing touches to *Tom Sawyer*. Before the close of the same year he had already begun work on *The Adventures of Huckleberry Finn,* published in 1885. It is interesting to note the use of the title, the "Duke of Bilgewater," in *Huck Finn* when the "Duchess of Bilgewater" had already made her appearance in *1601*. Sandwiched between his two great masterpieces, *Tom Sawyer* and *Huck Finn,* the writing of *1601* was indeed a strange interlude.

During this prolific period Mark wrote many minor items, most of them rejected by Howells, and read extensively in one of his favorite books, *Pepys' Diary*. Like many another writer Mark was captivated by Pepys' style and spirit, and "he determined," says Albert Bigelow Paine in his *Mark Twain, A Biography,* "to try his hand on an imaginary record of conversation and court manners of a bygone day, written in the phrase of the period. The result was *Fireside Conversation in the Time of Queen Elizabeth,* or as he later called it, *1601*. The 'conversation' recorded by a supposed Pepys of that period, was written with all the outspoken coarseness and nakedness of that rank day, when fireside sociabilities were limited only to the loosened fancy, vocabulary, and physical performance, and not by any bounds of convention."

"It was written as a letter," continues Paine, "to that robust divine, Rev. Joseph Twichell," who, unlike Howells, had no scruples about Mark's 'Elizabethan breadth of parlance.' "

The Rev. Joseph Twichell, Mark's most intimate friend for over forty years, was pastor of the Asylum Hill Congregational Church of Hartford, which Mark facetiously called the "Church of the Holy Speculators," because of its wealthy parishioners. Here Mark had first met "Joe" at a social, and their meeting ripened into a glorious, life-long friendship. Twichell was a man of about Mark's own age, a profound scholar, a devout Christian, "yet a man with an exuberant sense of humor, and a profound understanding of the frailties of mankind." The Rev. Mr. Twichell performed the marriage ceremony for Mark Twain and solemnized the births of his children; "Joe," his friend, counseled him on literary as well as personal matters for the remainder of Mark's life. It is important to catch this brief glimpse of the man for whom this masterpiece was written, for without it one can not fully understand the spirit in which *1601* was written, or the keen enjoyment which Mark and "Joe" derived from it.

"Save me one."

The story of the first issue of *1601* is one of finesse, state diplomacy, and surreptitious printing.

The Rev. "Joe" Twichell, for whose delectation the piece had been written, apparently had pocketed the document for four long years. Then, in 1880, it came into the hands of John Hay, later Secretary of State, presumably sent to him by Mark Twain. Hay pronounced the sketch a masterpiece, and wrote immediately to his old Cleveland friend, Alexander Gunn, prince of connoisseurs in art and literature. The following correspondence reveals the fine diplomacy which made the name of John Hay known throughout the world:

DEPARTMENT OF STATE
Washington

June 21, 1880.

Dear Gunn:

Are you in Cleveland for all this week? If you will say yes by return mail, I have a masterpiece to submit to your consideration which is only in my hands for a few days.

Yours, very much worritted by the depravity of Christendom,

Hay

The second letter discloses Hay's own high opinion of the effort and his deep concern for its safety.

June 24, 1880

My dear Gunn:

Here it is. It was written by Mark Twain in a serious effort to bring back our literature and philosophy to the sober and chaste Elizabethan standard. But the taste of the present day is too corrupt for anything so classic. He has not yet been able even to find a publisher. The Globe has not yet recovered from Downey's inroad, and they won't touch it.

I send it to you as one of the few lingering relics of that race of appreciative critics, who know a good thing when they see it.

Read it with reverence and gratitude and send it back to me; for Mark is impatient to see once more his wandering offspring.

Yours,
Hay.

In his third letter one can almost hear Hay's chuckle in the certainty that his diplomatic, if somewhat wicked, suggestion would bear fruit.

Washington, D. C.
July 7, 1880

My dear Gunn:

I have your letter, and the proposition which you make to pull a few proofs of the masterpiece is highly attractive, and of course highly immoral. I cannot properly consent to it, and I am afraid the great many would think I was taking an unfair advantage of his confidence. Please send back the document as soon as you can, and if, in spite of my prohibition, you take these proofs, save me one.

Very truly yours,
John Hay.

Thus was this Elizabethan dialogue poured into the moulds of cold type. According to Merle Johnson, Mark Twain's bibliographer, it was issued in pamphlet form, without wrappers or covers; there were 8 pages of text and the pamphlet measured 7 by 8½ inches. Only four copies are believed to have been printed, one for Hay, one for Gunn, and two for Twain.

"In the matter of humor," wrote Clemens, referring to Hay's delicious notes, "what an unsurpassable touch John Hay had!"

Humor at West Point

The first printing of *1601* in actual book form was "Donne at ye Academie Press, in 1882, West Point, New York, under the supervision of Lieut. C. E. S. Wood, then adjutant of the U. S. Military Academy.

In 1882 Mark Twain and Joe Twichell visited their friend Lieut. Wood at West Point, where they learned that Wood, as Adjutant, had under his control a small printing establishment. On Mark's return to Hartford, Wood received a letter asking if he would do Mark a great favor by printing something he had written, which he did not care to entrust to the ordinary printer. Wood replied that he would be glad to oblige. On April 3, 1882, Mark sent the manuscript:

"I enclose the original of 1603 [*sic*] as you suggest. I am afraid there are errors in it, also, heedlessness in antiquated spelling—e's stuck on often at end of words where they are not strickly necessary, etc.... I would go through the manuscript but I am too much driven just now, and it is not important anyway. I wish you would do me the kindness to make any and all corrections that suggest themselves to you.

Sincerely yours,

S. L. Clemens."

In 1925 Charles Erskine Scott Wood recalled in a foreword, which he wrote for the limited edition of *1601* issued by the Grabhorn Press, how he felt when he first saw the original manuscript. "When I read it," writes Wood, "I felt that the character of it would be carried a little better by a printing which pretended to the eye that it was contemporaneous with the pretended 'conversation.'

"I wrote Mark that for literary effect I thought there should be a species of forgery, though of course there was no effort to actually deceive a scholar. Mark answered that I might do as I liked;—that his only object was to secure a number of copies, as the demand for it was becoming burdensome, but he would be very grateful for any interest I brought to the doing.

"Well, Tucker [foreman of the printing shop] and I soaked some handmade linen paper in weak coffee, put it as a wet bundle into a warm room to mildew, dried it to a dampness approved by Tucker and he printed the 'copy' on a hand press. I had special punches cut for such Elizabethan abbreviations as the ä, ë, ö and ü, when followed by *m* or *n*—and for *the* (commonly and stupidly pronounced ye).

"The only editing I did was as to the spelling and a few old English words introduced. The spelling, if I remember correctly, is mine, but the text is exactly as written by Mark. I wrote asking his view of making the spelling of the period and he was enthusiastic—telling me to do whatever I thought best and he was greatly pleased with the result."

Thus was printed in a de luxe edition of fifty copies the most curious masterpiece of American humor, at one of America's most dignified institutions, the United States Military Academy at West Point.

"*1601* was so be-praised by the archaeological scholars of a quarter of a century ago," wrote Clemens in his letter to Charles Orr, "that I was rather inordinately vain of it. At that time it had been privately printed in several countries, among them Japan. A sumptuous edition on large paper, rough-edged, was made by Lieut. C. E. S. Wood at West Point—an edition of 50 copies—and distributed among popes and kings and such people. In England copies of that issue were worth twenty guineas when I was there six years ago, and none to be had."

From the Depths

Mark Twain's irreverence should not be misinterpreted: it was an irreverence which bubbled up from a deep, passionate insight into the well-springs of human nature. In *1601*, as in *The Man That Corrupted Hadleyburg,* and in *The Mysterious Stranger,* he tore the masks off human beings and left them cringing before the public view. With the deftness of a master surgeon Clemens dealt with human emotions and delighted in exposing human nature in the raw.

The spirit and the language of the *Fireside Conversation* were rooted deep in Mark Twain's nature and in his life, as C. E. S. Wood, who printed *1601* at West Point, has pertinently observed,

"If I made a guess as to the intellectual ferment out of which *1601* rose I would say that Mark's intellectual structure and subconscious graining was from Anglo-Saxons as primitive as the common man of the Tudor period. He came from the banks of the Mississippi—from the flatboatmen, pilots, roustabouts, farmers and village folk of a rude, primitive people—as Lincoln did.

"He was finished in the mining camps of the West among stage drivers, gamblers and the men of '49. The simple roughness of a frontier people was in his blood and brain.

"Words vulgar and offensive to other ears were a common language to him. Anyone who ever knew Mark heard him use them freely, forcibly, picturesquely in his unrestrained conversation. Such language is forcible as all primitive words are. Refinement seems to make for weakness—or let us say a cutting edge—but the old vulgar monosyllabic words bit like the blow of a pioneer's ax—and Mark was like that. Then I think *1601* came out of Mark's instinctive humor, satire and hatred of puritanism. But there is more than this; with all its humor there is a sense of real delight in what may be called obscenity for its own sake. Whitman and the Bible are no more obscene than Nature herself—no more obscene than a manure pile, out of which come roses and cherries. Every word used in *1601* was used by our own rude pioneers as a part of their vocabulary—and no word was ever invented by man with obscene intent, but only as language to express his meaning. No act of nature is obscene in itself—but when such words and acts are dragged in for an ulterior purpose they become offensive, as everything out of place is offensive. I think he delighted, too, in shocking—giving resounding slaps on what Chaucer would quite simply call 'the bare erse.' "

Quite aside from this Chaucerian "erse" slapping, Clemens had also a semi-serious purpose, that of reproducing a past time as he saw it in Shakespeare, Dekker, Jonson, and other writers of the Elizabethan era. *Fireside Conversation* was an exercise in scholarship illumined by a keen sense of character. It was made especially effective by the artistic arrangement of widely-gathered material into a compressed picture of a phase of the manners and even the minds of the men and women "in the spacious times of great Elizabeth."

Mark Twain made of *1601* a very smart and fascinating performance, carried over almost to grotesqueness just to show it was not done for mere delight in the frank naturalism of the functions with which it deals. That Mark Twain had made considerable study of this frankness is apparent from chapter four of *A Yankee At King Arthur's Court*, where he refers to the conversation at the famous Round Table thus:

"Many of the terms used in the most matter-of-fact way by this great assemblage of the first ladies and gentlemen of the land would have made a Comanche blush. Indelicacy is too mild a term to convey the idea. However, I had read *Tom Jones* and *Roderick Random* and other books of that kind and knew that the highest and first ladies and gentlemen in England had remained little or no cleaner in their talk, and in the morals and conduct which such talk implies, clear up to one hundred years ago; in fact clear into our own nineteenth century—in which century, broadly speaking, the earliest samples of the real lady and the real gentleman discoverable in English history,—or in European history, for that matter—may be said to have made their appearance. Suppose Sir Walter [Scott] instead of putting the conversation into the mouths of his characters, had allowed the characters to speak for themselves? We should have had talk from Rebecca and Ivanhoe and the soft lady Rowena which would embarrass a tramp in our day. However, to the unconsciously indelicate all things are delicate."

Mark Twain's interest in history and in the depiction of historical periods and characters is revealed through his fondness for historical reading in preference to fiction, and through his other historical writings. Even in the hilarious, youthful days in San Francisco, Paine reports that "Clemens, however, was never quite ready for sleep. Then, as ever, he would prop himself up in bed, light his pipe, and lose himself in English or French history until his sleep conquered." Paine tells us, too, that Lecky's *European Morals* was an old favorite.

The notes to *The Prince and the Pauper* show again how carefully Clemens examined his historical background, and his interest in these materials. Some of the more important sources are noted: Hume's *History of England,* Timbs' *Curiosities of London,* J. Hammond Trumbull's *Blue Laws, True and False.* Apparently Mark Twain relished it, for as Bernard DeVoto points out, "The book is always Mark Twain. Its parodies of Tudor speech lapse sometimes into a callow satisfaction in that idiom—Mark hugely enjoys his nathlesses and beshrews and marrys." The writing of *1601* foreshadows his fondness for this treatment.

> *"Do you suppose the liberties and the Brawn of These States have to do only with delicate lady-words? with gloved gentleman words?"*
>
> Walt Whitman, *An American Primer.*

Although *1601* was not matched by any similar sketch in his published works, it was representative of Mark Twain the man. He was no emaciated literary tea-tosser. Bronzed and weatherbeaten son of the West, Mark was a man's man, and that significant fact is emphasized by the several phases of Mark's rich life as steamboat pilot, printer, miner, and frontier journalist.

On the Virginia City *Enterprise* Mark learned from editor R. M. Daggett that "when it was necessary to call a man names, there were no expletives too long or too expressive to be hurled in rapid succession to emphasize the utter want of character of the man assailed. . . . There were typesetters there who could hurl anathemas at bad copy which would have frightened a Bengal tiger. The news editor could damn a mutilated dispatch in twenty-four languages."

In San Francisco in the sizzling sixties we catch a glimpse of Mark Twain and his buddy, Steve Gillis, pausing in doorways to sing "The Doleful Ballad of the Neglected Lover," an old piece of uncollected erotica. One morning, when a dog began to howl, Steve awoke "to find his room-mate standing in the door that opened out into a back garden, holding a big revolver, his hand shaking with cold and excitement," relates Paine in his *Biography*.

" 'Come here, Steve,' he said. 'I'm so chilled through I can't get a bead on him.'

" 'Sam,' said Steve, 'don't shoot him. Just swear at him. You can easily kill him at any range with your profanity.'

"Steve Gillis declares that Mark Twain let go such a scorching, singeing blast that the brute's owner sold him the next day for a Mexican hairless dog."

Nor did Mark's "geysers of profanity" cease spouting after these gay and youthful days in San Francisco. With Clemens it may truly be said that profanity was an art—a pyrotechnic art that entertained nations.

"It was my duty to keep buttons on his shirts," recalled Katy Leary, life-long housekeeper and friend in the Clemens ménage, "and he'd swear something terrible if I didn't. If he found a shirt in his drawer without a button on, he'd take every single shirt out of that drawer and throw them right out of the window, rain or shine—out of the bathroom window they'd go. I used to look out every morning to see the snowflakes—anything white. Out they'd fly! . . . Oh! he'd swear at anything when he was on a rampage. He'd swear at his razor if it didn't cut right, and Mrs. Clemens used to send me around to the bathroom door sometimes to knock and ask him what was the matter. Well, I'd go and knock; I'd say, 'Mrs. Clemens wants to know what's the matter.' And then he'd say to me (kind of low) in a whisper like, 'Did she hear me Katy?' 'Yes,' I'd say, 'every word.' Oh, well, he was ashamed then, he was afraid of getting scolded for swearing like that, because Mrs. Clemens hated swearing." But his swearing never seemed really bad to Katy Leary, "It was sort of funny, and a part of him, somehow," she said. "Sort of amusing it was—and gay—not like real swearing, 'cause he swore like an angel."

In his later years at Stormfield Mark loved to play his

favorite billiards. "It was sometimes a wonderful and fearsome thing to watch Mr. Clemens play billiards," relates Elizabeth Wallace. "He loved the game, and he loved to win, but he occasionally made a very bad stroke, and then the varied, picturesque, and unorthodox vocabulary, acquired in his more youthful years, was the only thing that gave him comfort. Gently, slowly, with no profane inflexions of voice, but irresistibly as though they had the headwaters of the Mississippi for their source, came this stream of unholy adjectives and choice expletives."

Mark's vocabulary ran the whole gamut of life itself. In Paris, in his appearance in 1879 before the Stomach Club, a jolly lot of gay wags, Mark's address, reports Paine, "obtained a wide celebrity among the clubs of the world, though no line of it, not even its title, has ever found its way into published literature." It is rumored to have been called "Some Remarks on the Science of Onanism."

In Berlin, Mark asked Henry W. Fisher to accompany him on an exploration of the Berlin Royal Library, where the librarian, having learned that Clemens had been the Kaiser's guest at dinner, opened the secret treasure chests for the famous visitor. One of these guarded treasures was a volume of grossly indecent verses by Voltaire, addressed to Frederick the Great. "Too much is enough," Mark is reported to have said, when Fisher translated some of the verses, "I would blush to remember any of these stanzas except to tell Krafft-Ebing about them when I get to Vienna." When Fisher had finished copying a verse for him Mark put it into his pocket, saying, "Livy [Mark's wife, Olivia] is so busy mispronouncing German these days she can't even attempt to get at this."

In his letters, too, Howells observed, "He had the Southwestern, the Lincolnian, the Elizabethan breadth of parlance, which I suppose one ought not to call coarse without calling one's self prudish; and I was often hiding away

in discreet holes and corners the letters in which he had
loosed his bold fancy to stoop on rank suggestion; I could
not bear to burn them, and I could not, after the first reading, quite bear to look at them. I shall best give my feeling
on this point by saying that in it he was Shakespearean."

"With a nigger squat on her safety-valve"

John Hay, Pike County Ballads.

"Is there any other explanation," asks Van Wyck
Brooks, "'of his Elizabethan breadth of parlance?' Mr.
Howells confesses that he sometimes blushed over Mark
Twain's letters, that there were some which, to the very
day when he wrote his eulogy on his dead friend, he could
not bear to reread. Perhaps if he had not so insisted, in
former years, while going over Mark Twain's proofs, upon
'having that swearing out in an instant,' he would never had
had cause to suffer from his having 'loosed his bold fancy to
stoop on rank suggestion.' Mark Twain's verbal Rabelai-
sianism was obviously the expression of that vital sap which,
not having been permitted to inform his work, had been
driven inward and left there to ferment. No wonder he was
always indulging in orgies of forbidden words. Consider
the famous book, *1601*, that *fireside conversation in the time
of Queen Elizabeth*: is there any obsolete verbal indecency
in the English language that Mark Twain has not pains-
takingly resurrected and assembled there? He, whose blood
was in constant ferment and who could not contain within
the narrow bonds that had been set for him the roitous exub-
erance of his nature, had to have an escape-valve, and he
poured through it a fetid stream of meaningless obscenity
—the waste of a priceless psychic material!" Thus, Brooks
lumps *1601* with Mark Twain's "bawdry," and interprets
it simply as another indication of frustration.

Figs for Fig Leaves!

Of course, the writing of such a piece as *1601* raised the
question of freedom of expression for the creative artist.

Although little discussed at that time, it was a question which intensely interested Mark, and for a fuller appreciation of Mark's position one must keep in mind the year in which *1601* was written, 1876. There had been nothing like it before in American literature; there had appeared no Caldwells, no Faulkners, no Hemingways. Victorian England was gushing Tennyson. In the United States polite letters was a cult of the Brahmins of Boston, with William Dean Howells at the helm of the *Atlantic*. Louisa May Alcott published *Little Women* in 1868-69, and *Little Men* in 1871. In 1873 Mark Twain led the van of the debunkers, scraping the gilt off the lily in the *Gilded Age.*

In 1880 Mark took a few pot shots at license in Art and Literature in his *Tramp Abroad,* "I wonder why some things are? For instance, Art is allowed as much indecent license to-day as in earlier times—but the privileges of Literature in this respect have been sharply curtailed within the past eighty or ninety years. Fielding and Smollet could portray the beastliness of their day in the beastliest language; we have plenty of foul subjects to deal with in our day, but we are not allowed to approach them very near, even with nice and guarded forms of speech. But not so with Art. The brush may still deal freely with any subject; however revolting or indelicate. It makes a body ooze sarcasm at every pore, to go about Rome and Florence and see what this last generation has been doing with the statues. These works, which had stood in innocent nakedness for ages, are all fig-leaved now. Yes, every one of them. Nobody noticed their nakedness before, perhaps; nobody can help noticing it now, the fig-leaf makes it so conspicuous. But the comical thing about it all, is, that the fig-leaf is confined to cold and pallid marble, which would be still cold and unsuggestive without this sham and ostentatious symbol of modesty, whereas warm-blooded paintings which do really need it have in no case been furnished with it.

"At the door of the Ufizzi, in Florence, one is confronted by statues of a man and a woman, noseless, battered, black with accumulated grime—they hardly suggest human beings—yet these ridiculous creatures have been thoughtfully and conscientiously fig-leaved by this fastidious generation. You enter, and proceed to that most-visited little gallery that exists in the world . . . and there, against the wall, without obstructing rag or leaf, you may look your fill upon the foulest, the vilest, the obscenest picture the world possesses—Titian's Venus. It isn't that she is naked and stretched out on a bed—no, it is the attitude of one of her arms and hand. If I ventured to describe the attitude, there would be a fine howl—but there the Venus lies, for anybody to gloat over that wants to—and there she has a right to lie, for she is a work of art, and Art has its privileges. I saw young girls stealing furtive glances at her; I saw young men gaze long and absorbedly at her; I saw aged, infirm men hang upon her charms with a pathetic interest. How I should like to describe her—just to see what a holy indignation I could stir up in the world—just to hear the unreflecting average man deliver himself about my grossness and coarseness, and all that.

"In every gallery in Europe there are hideous pictures of blood, carnage, oozing brains, putrefaction—pictures portraying intolerable suffering—pictures alive with every conceivable horror, wrought out in dreadful detail—and similar pictures are being put on the canvas every day and publicly exhibited—without a growl from anybody—for they are innocent, they are inoffensive, being works of art. But suppose a literary artist ventured to go into a painstaking and elaborate description of one of these grisly things —the critics would skin him alive. Well, let it go, it cannot be helped; Art retains her privileges, Literature has lost hers. Somebody else may cipher out the whys and the wherefores and the consistencies of it—I haven't got time."

Unfortunately, *1601* has recently been tagged by Professor Edward Wagenknecht as "the most famous piece of pornography in American literature." Like many another uninformed, Prof. W. is like the little boy who is shocked to see "naughty" words chalked on the back fence, and thinks they are pornography. The initiated, after years of wading through the mire, will recognize instantly the significant difference between filthy filth and funny "filth." Dirt for dirt's sake is something else again. Pornography, an eminent American jurist has pointed out, is distinguished by the "leer of the sensualist."

"The words which are criticised as dirty," observed Justice John M. Woolsey in the United States District Court of New York, lifting the ban on *Ulysses* by James Joyce, "are old Saxon words known to almost all men and, I venture, to many women, and are such words as would be naturally and habitually used, I believe, by the types of folk whose life, physical and mental, Joyce is seeking to describe." Neither was there "pornographic intent," according to Justice Woolsey, nor was *Ulysses* obscene within the legal definition of that word.

"The meaning of the word 'obscene,'" the Justice indicated, "as legally defined by the courts is: tending to stir the sex impulses or to lead to sexually impure and lustful thoughts.

"Whether a particular book would tend to excite such impulses and thoughts must be tested by the court's opinion as to its effect on a person with average sex instincts—what the French would call *l'homme moyen sensuel*—who plays, in this branch of legal inquiry, the same role of hypothetical reagent as does the 'reasonable man' in the law of torts and 'the learned man in the art' on questions of invention in patent law."

27

Obviously, it is ridiculous to say that the "leer of the sensualist" lurks in the pages of Mark Twain's *1601*.

A Droll Story

"In a way," observed William Marion Reedy, "*1601* is to Twain's whole works what the *Droll Stories* are to Balzac's. It is better than the privately circulated ribaldry and vulgarity of Eugene Field; is, indeed, an essay in a sort of primordial humor such as we find in Rabelais, or in the plays of some of the lesser stars that drew their light from Shakespeare's urn. It is humor or fun such as one expects, let us say, from the peasants of Thomas Hardy, outside of Hardy's books. And, though it be filthy, it yet hath a splendor of mere animalism of good spirits . . . I would say it is scatalogical rather than erotic, save for one touch toward the end. Indeed, it seems more of Rabelais than of Boccaccio or Masuccio or Aretino—is brutally British rather than lasciviously latinate, as to the subjects, but sumptuous as regards the language."

Immediately upon first reading, John Hay, later Secretary of State, had proclaimed *1601* a masterpiece. Albert Bigelow Paine, Mark Twain's biographer, likewise acknowledged its greatness, when he said, "*1601* is a genuine classic, as classics of that sort go. It is better than the gross obscenities of Rabelais, and perhaps in some day to come, the taste that justified *Gargantua* and the *Decameron* will give this literary refugee shelter and setting among the more conventional writing of Mark Twain. Human taste is a curious thing; delicacy is purely a matter of environment and point of view."

"It depends on who writes a thing whether it is coarse or not," wrote Clemens in his notebook in 1879. "I built a conversation which could have happened—I used words such as *were* used at that time—1601. I sent it anonymously to a magazine, and how the editor abused it and the sender!

But that man was a praiser of Rabelais and had been saying, 'O that we had a Rabelais!' I judged that I could furnish him one.

"Then I took it to one of the greatest, best and most learned of Divines [Rev. Joseph H. Twichell] and read it to him. He came within an ace of killing himself with laughter (for between you and me the thing *was* dreadfully funny. I don't often write anything that I laugh at myself, but I can hardly think of that thing without laughing). That old Divine said it was a piece of the finest kind of literary art—and David Gray of the Buffalo *Courier* said it ought to be printed privately and left behind me when I died, and then my fame as a literary artist would last."

FRANKLIN J. MEINE

Chicago, Illinois
December 25, 1938

The First Printing

Verbatim Reprint

[Date, 1601.]

CONVERSATION, AS IT WAS BY THE SOCIAL FIRESIDE, IN THE TIME OF THE TUDORS.

[MEM.—The following is supposed to be an extract from the diary of the Pepys of that day, the same being Queen Elizabeth's cup-bearer. He is supposed to be of ancient and noble lineage; that he despises these literary canaille; that his soul consumes with wrath, to see the queen stooping to talk with such; and that the old man feels that his nobility is defiled by contact with Shakespeare, etc., and yet he has *got* to stay there till her Majesty chooses to dismiss him.]

toke her maiste ye queene a fantasie such as she sometimes hath, and had to her closet certain that doe write playes, bokes, and such like, these being my lord Bacon, his worship Sir Walter Ralegh, Mr. Ben Jonson, and ye child Francis Beaumonte, which being but sixteen, hath yet turned his hand to ye doing of ye Lattin masters into our Englishe tong, with grete discretion and much applaus. Also came with these ye famous Shaxpur. A righte straunge mixing truly of mighty blode with mean, ye more in especial since ye queenes grace was present, as likewise these following, to wit: Ye Duchess of Bilgewater, twenty-two yeres of age; ye Countesse of Granby, twenty-six; her doter, ye Lady Helen, fifteen; as also these two maides of honor, to-wit, ye Lady Margery Boothy, sixty-five, and ye Lady Alice Dilberry, turned seventy, she being two yeres ye queenes graces elder.

I being her maites cup-bearer, had no choice but to remaine and beholde rank forgot, and ye high holde converse wh ye low as uppon equal termes, a grete scandal did ye world heare thereof.

In ye heat of ye talk it befel yt one did breake wind, yielding an exceding mightie and distresfull stink, whereat all did laugh full sore, and then—

Ye Queene.—Verily in mine eight and sixty yeres have I not heard the fellow to this fart. Meseemeth, by ye grete sound and clamour of it, it was male; yet ye belly it did lurk behinde shoulde now fall lean and flat against ye spine of him yt hath bene delivered of so stately and so vaste a bulk, where as ye guts of them yt doe quiff-splitters bear, stand comely still and rounde. Prithee let ye author confess ye offspring. Will my Lady Alice testify?

Lady Alice.—Good your grace, an' I had room for such a thundergust within mine ancient bowels, 'tis not in reason I coulde discharge ye same and live to thank God

33

for yt He did choose handmaid so humble whereby to shew his power. Nay, 'tis not I yt have broughte forth this rich o'ermastering fog, this fragrant gloom, so pray you seeke ye further.

Ye Queene.—Mayhap ye Lady Margery hath done ye companie this favor?

Lady Margery.—So please you madam, my limbs are feeble wh ye weighte and drouth of five and sixty winters, and it behoveth yt I be tender unto them. In ye good providence of God, an' *I* had contained this wonder, forsoothe wolde I have gi'en 'ye whole evening of my sinking life to ye dribbling of it forth, with trembling and uneasy soul, not launched it sudden in its matchless might, taking mine own life with violence, rending my weak frame like rotten rags. It was not I, your maisty.

Ye Queene.—O' God's name, who hath favored us? Hath it come to pass yt a fart shall fart *itself?* Not such a one as this, I trow. Young Master Beaumont—but no; 'twould have wafted him to heaven like down of goose's boddy. 'Twas not ye little Lady Helen—nay, ne'er blush, my child; thoul't tickle thy tender maidenhedde with many a mousie-squeak before thou learnest to blow a harricane like this. Wasn't you, my learned and ingenious Jonson?

Jonson.—So fell a blast hath ne'er mine ears saluted, nor yet a stench so all-pervading and immortal. 'Twas not a novice did it, good your maisty, but one of veteran experience—else hadde he failed of confidence. In sooth it was not I.

Ye Queene.—My lord Bacon?

Lord Bacon.—Not from my leane entrailes hath this prodigy burst forth, so please your grace. Naught doth so befit ye grete as grete performance; and haply shall ye finde yt 'tis not from mediocrity this miracle hath issued.

[Tho' ye subjoct be but a fart, yet will this tedious sink of learning pondrously phillosophize. Meantime did the foul and deadly stink pervade all places to that degree,

34

yt never smelt I ye like, yet dare I not to leave ye presence, albeit I was like to suffocate.]

Ye Queene.—What saith ye worshipful Master Shaxpur?

Shaxpur.—In the great hand of God I stand and so proclaim mine innocence. Though ye sinless hosts of heaven had foretold ye coming of this most desolating breath, proclaiming it a work of uninspired man, its quaking thunders, its firmament-clogging rottenness his own achievement in due course of nature, yet had not I believed it; but had said the pit itself hath furnished forth the stink, and heaven's artillery hath shook the globe in admiration of it.

[Then was there a silence, and each did turn him toward the worshipful Sr Walter Ralegh, that browned, embattled, bloody swash-buckler, who rising up did smile, and simpering say]—

Sr W.—Most gracious maisty, 'twas I that did it, but indeed it was so poor and frail a note, compared with such as I am wont to furnish, yt in sooth I was ashamed to call the weakling mine in so august a presence. It was nothing —less than nothing, madam—I did it but to clear my nether throat; but had I come prepared, then had I delivered something worthy. Bear with me, please your grace, till I can make amends.

[Then delivered he himself of such a godless and rock-shivering blast that all were fain to stop their ears, and following it did come so dense and foul a stink that that which went before did seem a poor and trifling thing beside it. Then saith he, feigning that he blushed and was confused, *I perceive that I am weak to-day, and cannot justice do unto my powers;* and sat him down as who should say, *There, it is not much yet he that hath an arse to spare, let him fellow that, an' he think he can.* By God, an' I were ye queene, I would e'en tip this swaggering braggart out o' the court, and let him air his grandeurs and break his intolerable wind before ye deaf and such as suffocation pleaseth.]

Then fell they to talk about ye manners and customs of many peoples, and Master Shaxpur spake of ye boke of ye sieur Michael de Montaine, wherein was mention of ye custom of widows of Perigord to wear uppon ye head-dress, in sign of widowhood, a jewel in ye similitude of a man's member wilted and limber, whereat ye queene did laugh and say widows in England doe wear prickes too, but betwixt the thighs, and not wilted neither, till coition hath done that office for them. Master Shaxpur did like-wise observe how yt ye sieur de Montaine hath also spoken of a certain emperor of such mighty prowess that he did take ten maidenheddes in ye compass of a single night, ye while his empress did entertain two and twenty lusty knights between her sheetes, yet was not satisfied; whereat ye merrie Countess Granby saith a ram is yet ye emperor's superior, sith he wil tup above a hundred yewes 'twixt sun and sun; and after, if he can have none more to shag, will masturbate until he hath enrich'd whole acres with his seed.

Then spake ye damned windmill, Sr Walter, of a peo-ple in ye uttermost parts of America, yt capulate not until they be five and thirty yeres of age, ye women being eight and twenty, and do it then but once in seven yeres.

Ye Queene.—How doth that like my little Lady Helen? Shall we send thee thither and preserve thy belly?

Lady Helen.—Please your highnesses grace, mine old nurse hath told me there are more ways of serving God than by locking the thighs together; yet am I willing to serve him yt way too, sith your highnesses grace hath set ye ensample.

Ye Queene.—God' wowndes a good answer, childe.

Lady Alice.—Mayhap 'twill weaken when ye hair sprouts below ye navel.

Lady Helen.—Nay, it sprouted two yeres syne; I can scarce more than cover it with my hand now.

Ye Queene.—Hear ye that, my little Beaumonte? Have ye not a little birde about ye that stirs at hearing tell of so sweete a neste?

Beaumonte.—'Tis not insensible, illustrious madam; but mousing owls and bats of low degree may not aspire to bliss so whelming and ecstatic as is found in ye downy nests of birdes of Paradise.

Ye Queene.—By ye gullet of God, 'tis a neat-turned compliment. With such a tongue as thine, lad, thou'lt spread the ivory thighs of many a willing maide in thy good time, an' thy cod-piece be as handy as thy speeche.

Then spake ye queene of how she met old Rabelais when she was turned of fifteen, and he did tell her of a man his father knew that had a double pair of bollocks, whereon a controversy followed as concerning the most just way to spell the word, ye contention running high betwixt ye learned Bacon and ye ingenious Jonson, until at last ye old Lady Margery, wearying of it all, saith, *Gentles, what mattereth it how ye shall spell the word? I warrant ye when ye use your bollocks ye shall not think of it; and my Lady Granby, be ye content; let the spelling be, ye shall enjoy the beating of them on your buttocks just the same, I trow. Before I had gained my fourteenth year I had learnt that them that would explore a cunt stop'd not to consider the spelling o't.*

Sr W.—In sooth, when a shift's turned up, delay is meet for naught but dalliance. Boccaccio hath a story of a priest that did beguile a maid into his cell, then knelt him in a corner to pray for grace to be rightly thankful for this tender maidenhead ye Lord had sent him; but ye abbot, spying through ye key-hole, did see a tuft of brownish hair with fair white flesh about it, wherefore when ye priest's prayer was done, his chance was gone, forasmuch as ye little maid had but ye one cunt, and that was already occupied to her content.

Then conversed they of religion, and ye mightie work ye old dead Luther did doe by ye grace of God. Then next about poetry, and Master Shaxpur did rede a part of his King Henry IV., ye which, it seemeth unto me, is not of ye value of an arsefull of ashes, yet they praised it bravely, one and all.

Ye same did rede a portion of his "Venus and Adonis," to their prodigious admiration, whereas I, being sleepy and fatigued withal, did deme it but paltry stuff, and was the more discomforted in that ye blody bucanier had got his wind again, and did turn his mind to farting with such villain zeal that presently I was like to choke once more. God damn this windy ruffian and all his breed. I wolde that hell mighte get him.

They talked about ye wonderful defense which old Sr. Nicholas Throgmorton did make for himself before ye judges in ye time of Mary; which was unlucky matter to broach, sith it fetched out ye quene with a *Pity yt he, having so much wit, had yet not enough to save his doter's maiden-hedde sound for her marriage-bed.* And ye quene did give ye damn'd Sr. Walter a look yt made hym wince—for she hath not forgot he was her own lover it yt olde day. There was silent uncomfortableness now; 'twas not a good turn for talk to take, sith if ye queene must find offense in a little harmless debauching, when pricks were stiff and cunts not loathe to take ye stiffness out of them, who of this company was sinless; behold, was not ye wife of Master Shaxpur four months gone with child when she stood uppe before ye altar? Was not her Grace of Bilgewater roger'd by four lords before she had a husband? Was not ye little Lady Helen born on her mother's wedding-day? And, beholde, were not ye Lady Alice and ye Lady Margery there, mouthing religion, whores from ye cradle?

In time came they to discourse of Cervantes, and of the new painter, Rubens, that is beginning to be heard of. Fine words and dainty-wrought phrases from the ladies now, one or two of them being, in other days, pupils of that poor ass, Lille, himself; and I marked how that Jonson and Shaxpur did fidget to discharge some venom of sarcasm, yet dared they not in the presence, the queene's grace being ye very flower of ye Euphuists herself. But behold, these be they yt, having a specialty, and admiring it in themselves, be jealous when a neighbor doth essaye it, nor can abide it in them long. Wherefore 'twas observable yt ye quene waxed uncontent; and in time labor'd grandiose speeche out of ye mouth of Lady Alice, who manifestly did mightily pride herself thereon, did quite exhauste ye quene's endurance, who listened till ye gaudy speeche was done, then lifted up her brows, and with vaste irony, mincing saith *O shit!* Whereat they alle did laffe, but not ye Lady Alice, yt olde foolish bitche.

Now was Sr. Walter minded of a tale he once did hear ye ingenious Margrette of Navarre relate, about a maid, which being like to suffer rape by an olde archbishoppe, did smartly contrive a device to save her maidenhedde, and said to him, *First, my lord, I prithee, take out thy holy tool and piss before me;* which doing, lo his member felle, and would not rise again.

The West Point Edition

in Facsimile

Conversation, as it was by the Social Fireside,

in the time of the Tudors.

[Mem.—The following is supposed to be an extract from the diary of the Pepys of that day, the same being cup-bearer to Queen Elizabeth.   It is supposed that he is of ancient and noble lineage ; that he despises these literary *canaille ;* that his soul consumes with wrath to see the Queen stooping to talk with such ; and that the old man feels his nobility defiled by contact with Shakspere, etc., and yet he has *got* to stay there till Her Majesty chooses to dismiss him.]

YESTERNIGHT toke her maieſtie ẙ queene a fan
taſie ſuch as ſhee ſometimes hath, & hadde to her
cloſet certaine ẙ doe write playes, bookes, & ſvch
like, theſe beeing my lord Bacon, his worſhip Sr.
Walter Ralegh, Mr. Ben Jonſon, & ẙ childe Francis Beaumonte, wch beeing but ſixteen, hath yet
turned his hãd to ẙ doing of ẙ Lattin maſters into our Englyche tong, with grete diſcretion&much
applaus.   Alſo came with theſe ẙ famous Shaxpur.   A righte straunge mixing truly of mighty
bloud with meã, ẙ more in eſpecial ſyns ẙ queenes
grace was preſent, as likewyſe theſe following, to
wit: Ye Ducheſſe of Bilgewater, twenty-two yeeres
of age ; ẙ Counteſſe of Granby, twenty-ſix ; her
doter, ẙ Lady Helen, fifteen ; as alſo theſe two
maides of honor, to wit : ẙ Lady Margery Boothy,
ſixty-fiue, & ẙ Lady Alice Dilberry, turned ſeuen-
ty, ſhee beeing two yeeres ẙ queenes graces elder.
    I   beeing her mai$^{sty's}$ cup-bearer, hadde no
choyce but to remayne & behold ranke forgotte, &
ẙ high holde conuerſe w^h ẙ low as uppon equal
termes, a grete ſcandal did ẙ world heare therof.
    In ẙ heat of ẙ talke it befel ẙ one did breake

wind, yielding an exceding mighty & diftrefsfull stink, whereat all did laffe full fore, and thẽ :

Ye Queene. Verily in mine eight and fixty yeeres have I not heard ẏ fellow to this fart. Me-seemeth, by ẏ grete sound and clamour of it, it was male ; yet ẏ belly it did lurk behinde fhoulde now fall lene & flat agaynft ẏ fpine of him ẏ hath beene delivered of fo ftately & fo vafte a bulke, whereas ẏ guts of them ẏ doe quiff-fplitters bear, ftand comely ftill & rounde.   Prithee, lette ẏ author confeffe ẏ offfpring. Wil my Lady Alice teftify ?

Lady Alice. Good your grace, an' I hadde room for such a thunderguft within mine auncient bow-els, 'tis not in reafon I coulde difcharge ẏ same & live to thanck God for ẏ Hee did chufe handmayd so humble whereby to shew his power.   Nay, 'tis not I ẏ have broughte forth yˢ ryche o'ermaftering fog, yˢ fragrant gloom,so pray you feeke ye further.

Ye Queene. Mayhap ẏ Lady Margery hath done ẏ companie this favour ?

Lady Margerey. So pleafe you madã,my limbs are feeble wʰ ẏ weighte and drouth of fiue & fixty winters, & it behoveth ẏ I be tender vnto thẽ. In ẏ good providence of God, an' *I* hadde contained yˢ wonder, forfoothe wolde I haue gi'en ẏ whole euening of my finking life to ẏ dribbling of it forth, w^h trembling & vneafy foul, not launched it fuddē in its matchleffe might, taking myne owne life with uiolence, rending my weak frame like rottē rags. It was not I, your mai^{sty}.

Ye Queene. O' God's naym, who hath favoured us? Hath it come to pafs ẏ a fart fhall fart *itfelfe?* Not foche a one as this, I trow. Young Mafter Beaumont; but no, 'twould have wafted him to Heav'n like down of goofe's boddy. 'Twas not ẏ little Lady Helen--nay, ne'er blufh, my child; thoul't tickle thy tender maidēhedde with many a moufie-fqueak before thou learneft to blow a harricane like this. Waf't you, my learned & ingenious Jonfon?

Jonfon. So fell a blaft hath ne'er mine ears saluted, nor yet a ftench fo all-pervading&immortal. 'Twas not a nouice did it, good your maieftie, but one of ueterā experiēce--elfe hadde hee fayled of confidence. In footh it was not I.

Ye Queene. My lord Bacon?

Lord Bacon. Not from my leāe ētrailes hath this prodigie burft forth, fo pleafe your grace. Nau't doth fo befit ẏ grete as grete performance; &haply fhall ye finde ẏ 'tis not from mediocrity this miracle hath iffued.

(Tho' ÿ fubject bee but a fart, yet will yˢ tedious fink of learning ponderoufly philofophize. Meantime did ÿ foul&deadly ftink peruade all places to ÿ degree, ÿ never fmelt I ÿ like, yet dared I not to leave ÿ prefẽce, albeit I was like to fuffocate.)

Ye Queene. What faith ÿ worfhipful Mafter Shaxpur?

Shaxpur. In ÿ grete hãd of God I ftand, & so proclaim my innocence. Tho'gh ÿ finlefs hofts of Heav'n hadde foretold ÿ comyng of yˢ moft defolating breath, proclaiming it a werke of uninfpired mã, its quaking thunders, its firmamẽt-clogging rottennefse his owne achievemẽt in due courfe of nature, yet hadde not I believed it; but hadde sayd ÿ pit itfelf hath furnifhed forth ÿ stink, & Heav'n's artillery hath shook ÿ globe in admiration of it.

(Thẽ was there a filence, & each did turne him toward ÿ worfhipful Sr Walter Ralegh, ÿ brown'd, embatteld, bloudy fwafhbuckler, who rifing vp did fmile, & fimpering, fay :)

Sr. W. Moft gracious maieftie, 'twas I ÿ did it, but indeed it was so poor & frail a note, compared with fuch as I ã wont to furnifh, ÿ in footh I was afhamed to call ÿ weakling mine in foe auguft a

preſēce. It was nothing--leſs thã nothing,madam,
I did it but to clere my nether throat ; but hadde
I come prepared thē hadde I delivered ſomething
worthy.   Bear with mee, pleaſe your grace, till I
can make amends.

(Thē delivered hee himſelfe of ſuch a godleſſe &
rocke-ſhivering blaſt ẙ all were fain to ſtop their
ears,& following it did come ſo denſe&foul a ſtink
ẙ that which went before did ſeeme a poor&trif-
ling thing beſide it.   Thē ſaith he, feigning ẙ he
bluſhed&was confuſed, *I perceive that I am weak
to-daie & cannot juſtice doe vnto my powers ;* &
ſat him down as who ſholde ſay, *There,it is not
moche ; yet he that hath an arse to spare lette
hym fellow that, an' hee think hee can.* ByGod,
an' I were ẙ queene,I wolde e'en tip yˢ ſwaggering
braggart ouᵗ o' the court,& lette him air his gran-
deurs&break his intolerable wynd before ye deaf&
ſuch as ſuffocation pleſeth.)

Thē fell they to talke about ẙ manners&cuſt'ms
of many peoples,&Maſter Shaxpur ſpake of ẙ booke
of ẙ ſieur Michael de Montaine,wherein was mention of ẙ couſtom of widows of Perigord to wear
vppon ẙ hedde-dreſs,in ſign of widowhood,a jewel
in ẙ ſimilitude of a man's mēber wilted & limber,

whereat ẙ queene did laffe&say,widows inEngland
doe wear prickes too, but 'twixt ẙ thyghs, & not
wilted neither,till coition hath done that office for
thẽ.   Mafter Shaxpur did likewife obferve how ẙ ẙ
fieur de Montaine hath alfo fpoken of a certaine
emperour of foche mightie proweffe ẙ hee did take
ten maidẽ-heddes in ẙ compafs of a fingle night,ẙ
while his empreffe did entertain two&twẽty lufty
knights atweene her fheetes,yet was not fatiffide ;
whereat ẙ merrie Counteffe Granby faith a ram is
yet ẙ emperour's fuperiour,fith hee wil tup above
an hundred yewes 'twixt funne&funne,&after,if ẙ
hee can have none more to fhag, wil mafturbate
until hee hath enrych'd whole acres wʰ hys feed.

Thẽ fpake ẙ damned wyndmill,SrWalter, of a
people ih ẙ vttermoft parts of America ẙ copulate
not vntil they be fiue-&-thirty yeeres of age,ẙwomẽ
beeing eight-&-twenty,& doe it thẽ but once in
fevẽ yeeres.

Ye Queene. How doth thatte like my lyttle
LadyHelen ? Shᵃˡˡ wee fend thee thither & preferve
thy belly ?

Lady Helen. Pleafe yʳ highneffes grace, mine
old nurfe hath told mee there bee more ways of
feruing God thã by locking ẙ thyghs together;yet

ã I willing to ſerue him ẏ way too,ſith yovr high-
neſſes grace hath ſet ẏ enſample.

Ye Queene. God's wowndes a goode anivver,
childe.

Lady Alice. Mayhap 'twill weakẽ whẽ ẏ hair
ſprouts below ẏ navel.

Lady Helen. Nay,it ſprouted two yeeres ſyne;
I can ſcarce more thã cover it with my hãd now.

Ye Queene. Hear ye thatte, my little Beaumonte? Have ye not a ſmalle birde about ye that
ſtirs at hearing tel of ſoe ſweete a neſte?

Beaumonte. 'Tis not inſêſible,illuſtrious madã;
but mouſing owls&bats of low degree may not aſ-
pire to bliſs ſoe whelming & ecſtatic as is found in
ẏ downie neſts of birdes of Paradiſe.

Ye Queene. By ẏ gullet of God, 'tis a neat-
turned complimẽt. With ſoche a tong as thyne,
lad,thou'lt spread the ivorie thyghs of many a wil-
ing mayd in thy good time, an' thy cod-piece bee
as handy as thy ſpeeche.

Thẽ ſpake ẏ queene of how ſhee met old Rabelais whẽ ſhee was turned of fifteen,& hee did tel
her of a man his father knew that hadde a double
pair of bollocks,whereon a controverſy followed as

concerning the moſt juſt way to ſpell ẏ word, ẏ contention running high 'twixt ẏ learned Bacon & ẏ
ingenious Jonſon, until at laſt ẏ old Lady Margery,
wearying of it all, ſaith, ,,Gentles, what mattereth
it how ye ſhal ſpell ẏ word? I warrãt ye whẽ ye
use y bollocks ye ſhall not think of it; & my Lady
Granby, bee ye content; lette ẏ ſpelling bee; you ſhal
enjoy ẏ beating of them on your buttocks juſt ẏ
ſame, I trow. Before I hadde gained my fourteenth
yeere I hadde learnt ẏ them ẏ would explore a cunt
ſtop'd not to conſider the ſpelling o't."

Sr W. In ſooth, whẽ a ſhift's turned upp delay is meet for naught but dalliance. Boccaccio
hath a ſtory of a prieſt ẏ did beguile a mayd into
his cell, thẽ knelt him in a corner for to pray for
grace ẏ hee bee rightly thanckfvll for y tẽder maid-
ẽhedde ẏ Lord hadde ſent him; but ẏ abbot ſpying
through ẏ key-hole, did ſee a tuft of browniſh hair
with fair white fleſh about it, wherefore whẽ ẏ
prieſt's prayer was donne, his chance was gone, for-
aſmuch as ẏ lyttle mayd hadde but ẏ one cunt, &
ẏ was already occupied to her content.

Thẽ converſed they of religion, & ẏ mightie
werke ẏ olde dead Luther did doe by ẏ grace of
God. Thẽ next about poetry, & Maſter Shaxpur
did rede a parte of his Kyng Henry iv, ẏ which,

it feemeth vnto mee,is not of ẙ ualve of an arfefvl of afhes,yet they praifed it bravely,one&all.

Y fame did rede a portion of his ,,Venvs & Adonis," to their prodigious admiration,vvhereas I, beeing fleepy & fatigved withal, did deme it but paltrie ftoffe,& was the more discomforted in ẙ ẙ bloudie bucanier hadde gotte his wynd again, & did turne his mind to farting with fuch uillain zeal ẙ prefently I was like to choke once more. God damn this wyndy ruffian&all his breed. I wolde ẙ hell mighte gette hym.

They talked about ẙ wonderful defenfe which olde Sr Nickolas Throgmorton did make for him-felfe before ẙ judges in ẙ time of Mary ; wᶜʰ was unlvcky matter for to broach, fith it fetched out ẙ queene with a *Pity yᵗ hee, hauing foe moche wit, hadde yet not enough to faue his doter's maiden hedde founde for her marriage-bedde.* And ẙ queene did give ẙ damn'd Sr.Walter a look ẙ made hym wince--for fhee hath not forgot hee was her own lover in ẙ olde daie. There was filent un-comfortableneſs now ; 'twas not a good turne for talk to take,fith if ẙ queene muft find offenfe in a little harmleſse debauching,when pricks were ftiff & cunts not loath to take ẙ ftiffneſs out of them, who of yˢ companie was finleſs ; beholde was not

51

ỹ wife of Mafter Shaxpur four months gone with child whẽ fhe ftood uppe before ỹ altar? Was not her Grace of Bilgewater roger'd by four lords before fhe hadde a hufband? Was not ỹ lyttle LadyHelen born on her mother's wedding-day? And, beholde, were not ỹ LadyAlice&ỹ LadyMargery there, mouthing religion, whores from ỹ cradle?

In time came they to difcourfe of Ceruãtes, & of ỹ new painter, Rubẽs, ỹ is begynning to bee heard of. Fine words & dainty-wrought phrafes from ỹ ladies now,one or two of them beeing, in other days, pupils of ỹ poor afs,Lille, himfelf; & I marked how ỹ Jonfon&Shaxpur did fidget to difcharge fome uenom of farcafm,yet dared they not in ỹ prefence, ỹ queene's grace beeing ỹ uery flower of ỹ Euphuifts herfelfe. But beholde,there bee they ỹ,having a fpecialtie, & admiring it in themfelues,bee jealous when a neighbour doth effaye it, nor can bide it in them long. Wherefore 'twas obfervable ỹ ỹ queene waxed uncontent; &in tyme a labor'd grandiofe fpeech out of ỹ mouthe of Lady Alice, who manifeftly did mightily pride herfelf thereon, did quite exhavfte ỹ queene's endurance, who listened till ỹ gaudy fpeeche was done, thẽ lifted up her brows, & with uafte irony, mincing ſayth, „*Oſhit !*" Whereat they all did laffe, but not ẙ LadyAlice,ẙ olde fooliſh bitche.

Now was Sr Walter minded of a tale hee once did hear ẙ ingenious Margrette of Navarre relate, about a maid,which beeing like to ſuffer rape by an olde archbiſhoppe,did ſmartly contriue a deuice to ſaue her maydẽhedde,&ſaid to him, „Firſt, my lord,I prithee, take out thy holy tool & piſs before mee," wch doing, lo hys member felle, &wolde not riſe again.   *Date 1601.*

DONE ATT

Y^e Academie Preſſe,
M DCCC LXXX II.

Footnotes

to Frivolity

The historical consistency of *1601* indicates that Twain must have given the subject considerable thought. The author was careful to speak only of men who conceivably might have been in the Virgin Queen's closet and engaged in discourse with her.

The Characters

At this time (1601) Queen Elizabeth was 68 years old. She speaks of having talked to "old Rabelais" in her youth. This might have been possible as Rabelais died in 1552, when the Queen was 19 years old.

Among those in the party were Shakespeare, at that time 37 years old; Ben Jonson, 27; and Sir Walter Raleigh, 49. Beaumont at the time was 17, not 16. He was admitted as a member of the Inner Temple in 1600, and his first translations, those from Ovid, were first published in 1602. Therefore, if one were holding strictly to the year date, neither by age nor by fame would Beaumont have been eligible to attend such a gathering of august personages in the year 1601; but the point is unimportant.

The Elizabethan Writers

In the *Conversation* Shakespeare speaks of Montaigne's *Essays*. These were first published in 1580 and successive editions were issued in the years following, the third volume being published in 1588. "In England Montaigne was early popular. It was long supposed that the autograph of Shakespeare in a copy of Florio's translation showed his study of the *Essays*. The autograph has been disputed, but divers passages, and especially one in *The Tempest,* show that at first or second hand the poet was acquainted with the essayist." (Encyclopedia Brittanica.)

The company at the Queen's fireside discoursed of Lilly (or Lyly), English dramatist and novelist of the Elizabethan era, whose novel, *Euphues,* published in two parts, *Euphues, or the Anatomy of Wit* (1579) and *Euphues and*

His England (1580) was a literary sensation. It is said to have influenced literary style for more than a quarter of a century, and traces of its influence are found in Shakespeare. (Columbia Encyclopedia).

The introduction of Ben Jonson into the party was wholly appropriate, if one may call to witness some of Jonson's writings. The subject under discussion was one that Jonson was acquainted with, in *The Alchemist:*

Act. 1, Scene 1,
FACE: Believe't I will.
SUBTLE: Thy worst. I fart at thee.
DOL COMMON: Have you your wits? Why, gentlemen, for love—

Act. 2, Scene 1,
SIR EPICURE MAMMON: . . . and then my poets, the same that writ so subtly of the fart, whom I shall entertain still for that subject.
and again in *Bartholomew Fair*
NIGHTENGALE: (sings a ballad)
Hear for your love, and buy for your money.
A delicate ballad o' the ferret and the coney.
A preservative again' the punk's evil.
Another goose-green starch, and the devil.
A dozen of divine points, and the godly garter
The fairing of good counsel, of an ell and three-quarters.
What is't you buy?
The windmill blown down by the witche's fart,
Or Saint George, that, O! did break the dragon's heart.

A Good Old English Custom

That certain types of English society have not changed materially in their freedom toward breaking wind in public can be noticed in some comparatively recent literature. Frank Harris in *My Life,* vol. 2, Ch. XIII, tells of Lady Marriott, wife of a Judge Advocate General, being compelled to leave her own table, at which she was entertaining Sir Robert Fowler, then the Lord Mayor of London, because of the suffocating and nauseating odors there. He also tells of an instance in parliament, and of a rather brilliant *bon mot* spoken upon that occasion.

"While Fowler was speaking Finch-Hatton had shewn signs of restlessness; towards the end of the speech he had moved some three yards away from the Baronet. As soon as Fowler sat down Finch-Hatton sprang up holding his handkerchief to his nose:

" 'Mr. Speaker,' he began, and was at once acknowledged by the Speaker, for it was a maiden speech, and as such was entitled to precedence by the courteous custom of the House, 'I know why the Right Honourable Member from the City did not conclude his speech with a proposal. The only way to conclude such a speech appropriately would be with a motion!' "

Aeolian Crepitations

But society had apparently degenerated sadly in modern times, and even in the era of Elizabeth, for at an earlier date it was a serious—nay, capital—offense to break wind in the presence of majesty. The Emperor Claudius, hearing that one who had suppressed the urge while paying him court had suffered greatly thereby, "intended to issue an edict, allowing to all people the liberty of giving vent at table to any distension occasioned by flatulence."

Martial, too (Book XII, Epigram LXXVII), tells of the embarrassment of one who broke wind while praying in the Capitol,

"One day, while standing upright, addressing his prayers to Jupiter, Aethon farted in the Capitol. Men laughed, but the Father of the Gods, offended, condemned the guilty one to dine at home for three nights. Since that time, miserable Aethon, when he wishes to enter the Capitol, goes first to Paterclius' privies and farts ten or twenty times.

Yet, in spite of this precautionary crepitation, he salutes Jove with constricted buttocks." Martial also (Book IV, Epigram LXXX), ridicules a woman who was subject to the habit, saying,

"Your Bassa, Fabullus, has always a child at her side, calling it her darling and her plaything; and yet—more wonder—she does not care for children. What is the reason then. Bassa is apt to fart. (For which she could blame the unsuspecting infant.)"

The tale is told, too, of a certain woman who performed an aeolian crepitation at a dinner attended by the witty Monsignieur Dupanloup, Bishop of Orleans, and that when, to cover up her lapse, she began to scrape her feet upon the floor, and to make similar noises, the Bishop said, "Do not trouble to find a rhyme, Madam!"

Nay, worthier names than those of any yet mentioned have discussed the matter. Herodotus tells of one such which was the precursor to the fall of an empire and a change of dynasty—that which Amasis discharges while on horseback, and bids the envoy of Apries, King of Egypt, catch and deliver to his royal master. Even the exact manner and posture of Amasis, author of this insult, is described.

St. Augustine (The City of God, XIV:24) cites the instance of a man who could command his rear trumpet to sound at will, which his learned commentator fortifies with the example of one who could do so *in tune!*

Benjamin Franklin, in his "Letter to the Royal Academy of Brussels" has canvassed suggested remedies for alleviating the stench attendant upon these discharges:

"My Prize Question therefore should be: *To discover some Drug, wholesome and not disagreeable, to be mixed with our common food, or sauces, that shall render the natural discharges of Wind from our Bodies not only inoffensive, but agreeable as Perfumes.*

"That this is not a Chimerical Project & altogether impossible, may appear from these considerations. That we already have some knowledge of means capable of *varying* that smell. He that dines on stale Flesh, especially with much Addition of Onions, shall be able to afford a stink that no Company can tolerate; while he that has lived for some time on Vegetables only, shall have that Breath so pure as to be insensible of the most delicate Noses; and if he can manage so as to avoid the Report, he may anywhere give vent to his Griefs, unnoticed. But as there are many to whom an entire Vegetable Diet would be inconvenient, & as a little quick Lime thrown into a Jakes will correct the amazing Quantity of fetid Air arising from the vast Mass of putrid Matter contained in such Places, and render it pleasing to the Smell, who knows but that a little Powder of Lime (or some other equivalent) taken in our Food, or perhaps a Glass of Lime Water drank at Dinner, may have the same Effect on the Air produced in and issuing from our Bowels?"

One curious commentary on the text is that Elizabeth should be so fond of investigating into the authorship of the exhalation in question, when she was inordinately fond of strong and sweet perfumes; in fact, she was responsible for the tremendous increase in importations of scents into England during her reign.

"Ye boke of ye sieur Michael de Montaine"

There is a curious admixture of error and misunderstanding in this part of the sketch. In the first place, the story is borrowed from Montaigne, where it is told inaccurately, and then further corrupted in the telling.

It was not the good widows of Perigord who wore the *phallus* upon their coifs; it was the young married women, of the district near Montaigne's home, who paraded it to view upon their foreheads, as a symbol, says our essayist, "of the joy they derived therefrom." If they became widows, they reversed its position, and covered it up with the rest of their head-dress.

The "emperor" mentioned was not an emperor; he was Procolus, a native of Albengue, on the Genoese coast, who, with Bonosus, led the unsuccessful rebellion in Gaul against Emperor Probus. Even so keen a commentator as Cotton has failed to note the error.

The empress (Montaigne does not say "his empress") was Messalina, third wife of the Emperor Claudius, who was uncle of Caligula and foster-father to Nero. Furthermore, in her case the charge is that she copulated with *twenty-five* in a single night, and not twenty-two, as appears in the text. Montaigne is right in his statistics, if original sources are correct, whereas the author erred in transcribing the incident.

As for Proculus, it has been noted that he was associated with Bonosus, who was as renowned in the field of Bacchus as was Proculus in that of Venus (Gibbon, Decline and Fall of the Roman Empire). The feat of Proculus is told in his own words, in Vopiscus, (*Hist. Augustine,* p. 246) where he recounts having captured one hundred Sarmatian virgins, and unmaidened ten of them in one night, together with the happenings subsequent thereto.

Concerning Messalina, there appears to be no question but that she was a nymphomaniac, and that, while Empress of Rome, she participated in some fearful debaucheries. The question is what to believe, for much that we have heard about her is almost certainly apocryphal.

The author from whom Montaigne took his facts is the elder Pliny, who, in his *Natural History,* Book X, Chapter 83, says, "Other animals become sated with veneral pleasures; man hardly knows any satiety. Messalina, the wife of Claudius Caesar, thinking this a palm quite worthy of an empress, selected for the purpose of deciding the question, one of the most notorious women who followed the profession of a hired prostitute; and the empress outdid her, after continuous intercourse, night and day, at the twenty-fifth embrace."

But Pliny, notwithstanding his great attainments, was often a retailer of stale gossip, and in like case was Aurelius Victor, another writer who heaped much odium on her name. Again, there is a great *hiatus* in the *Annals of Tacitus,* a true historian, at the period covering the earlier days of the Empress; while Suetonius, bitter as he may be, is little more than an anecdotist. Juvenal, another of her detractors, is a prejudiced witness, for he started out to satirize female vice, and naturally aimed at high places. Dio also tells of Messalina's misdeeds, but his work is under the same limitations as that of Suetonius. Furthermore, none but Pliny mentions the excess under consideration.

However, "where there is much smoke there must be a little fire," and based upon the superimposed testimony of the writers of the period, there appears little doubt but that Messalina was a nymphomaniac, that she prostituted herself in the public stews, naked, and with gilded nipples, and that she did actually marry her chief adulterer, Silius, while Claudius was absent at Ostia, and that the wedding was consummated in the presence of a concourse of witnesses. This was "the straw that broke the camel's back." Claudius hastened back to Rome, Silius was dispatched, and Messalina, lacking the will-power to destroy herself, was killed when an officer ran a sword through her abdomen, just as it appeared that Claudius was about to relent.

"Then spake ye damned windmill, Sir Walter"

Raleigh is thoroughly in character here; this observation is quite in keeping with the general veracity of his account of his travels in Guiana, one of the most mendacious accounts of adventure ever told. Naturally, the scholarly researches of Westermarck have failed to discover this people; perhaps Lady Helen might best be protected among the Jibaros of Ecuador, where the men marry when approaching forty.

Ben Jonson in his *Conversations* observed "That Sr.

W. Raughlye esteemed more of fame than of conscience."

Ye Virgin Queene

Grave historians have debated for centuries the pretensions of Elizabeth to the title, "The Virgin Queen," and it is utterly impossible to dispose of the issue in a note. However, the weight of opinion appears to be in the negative. Many and great were the difficulties attending the marriage of a Protestant princess in those troublous times, and Elizabeth finally announced that she would become wedded to the English nation, and she wore a ring in token thereof until her death. However, more or less open *liaisons* with Essex and Leicester, as well as a host of lesser courtiers, her ardent temperament, and her imperious temper, are indications that cannot be denied in determining any estimate upon the point in question.

Ben Jonson in his *Conversations* with William Drummond of Hawthornden says,

"Queen Elizabeth never saw herself after she became old in a true glass; they painted her, and sometymes would vermillion her nose. She had allwayes about Christmass evens set dice that threw sixes or five, and she knew not they were other, to make her win and esteame herself fortunate. That she had a membrana on her, which made her uncapable of man, though for her delight she tried many. At the comming over of Monsieur, there was a French Chirurgion who took in hand to cut it, yett fear stayed her, and his death."

It was a subject which again intrigued Clemens when he was abroad with W. H. Fisher, whom Mark employed to "nose up" everything pertaining to Queen Elizabeth's manly character.

"Boccaccio hath a story"

The author does not pay any great compliment to Raleigh's memory here. There is no such tale in all Boccaccio. The nearest related incident forms the subject matter

of Dineo's novel (the fourth) of the First day of the
Decameron.

Old Sr. Nicholas Throgmorton

The incident referred to appears to be Sir Nicholas
Throgmorton's trial for complicity in the attempt to make
Lady Jane Grey Queen of England, a charge of which he
was acquitted. This so angered Queen Mary that she im-
prisoned him in the Tower, and fined the jurors from one
to two thousand pounds each. Her action terrified succeed-
ing juries, so that Sir Nicholas's brother was condemned
on no stronger evidence than that which had failed to pre-
vail before. While Sir Nicholas's defense may have been
brilliant, it must be admitted that the evidence was weak.
He was later released from the Tower, and under Elizabeth
was one of a group of commissioners sent by that princess
into Scotland, to foment trouble with Mary, Queen of Scots.
When the attempt became known, Elizabeth repudiated the
acts of her agents, but Sir Nicholas, having anticipated this
possibility, had sufficient foresight to secure endorsement of
his plan by the Council, and so outwitted Elizabeth, who
was playing a two-faced role, and Cecil, one of the greatest
statesmen who ever held the post of principal minister.
Perhaps it was this incident to which the company referred,
which might in part explain Elizabeth's rejoinder. However, he had been restored to confidence ere this, and had
served as ambassador to France.

"To save his doter's maidenhedde"

Elizabeth Throckmorton (or Throgmorton), daughter
of Sir Nicholas, was one of Elizabeth's maids of honor.
When it was learned that she had been debauched by Raleigh, Sir Walter was recalled from his command at sea by
the Queen, and compelled to marry the girl. This was not
"in that olde daie," as the text has it, for it happened only
eight years before the date of this purported "conversation,"
when Elizabeth was sixty years old.

Bibliography

The various printings of *1601*
reveal how Mark Twain's *Fireside Conversation* has become a part of the American printer's lore. But more important, its many printings indicate that it has become a popular bit of American folklore, particularly for men and women who have a feeling for Mark Twain. Apparently it appeals to the typographer, who devotes to it his worthy art, as well as to the job printer, who may pull a crudely printed proof. The gay procession of curious printings of *1601* is unique in the history of American printing.

Indeed, the story of the various printings of *1601* is almost legendary. In the days of the "jour." printer, so I am told, well-thumbed copies were carried from print shop to print shop. For more than a quarter century now it has been one of the chief sources of enjoyment for printers' devils; and many a young rascal has learned about life from this *Fireside Conversation*. It has been printed all over the country, and if report is to be believed, in foreign countries as well. Because of the many surreptitious and anonymous printings it is exceedingly difficult, if not impossible, to compile a complete bibliography. Many printings lack the name of the publisher, the printer, the place or date of printing. In many instances some of the data, through the patient questioning of fellow collectors, has been obtained and supplied.

Karl Yost has pioneered in this field, and the present bibliography has drawn heavily upon his enthusiastic and intelligent bibliographic work. Mr. Yost has generously placed at my disposal his collection of *1601*'s and all his notes. Mr. Irvin Haas has continued the good work in his edition of *1601*, published by the Black Cat Press in 1936. The catalogue of the Willard S. Morse collection of Twainiana has also been made available through the courtesy of George H. Brownell. From these sources and my own materials and notes I have compiled the following bibliography, knowing full well that it cannot be complete, but hoping that it will at least contribute to the enjoyment of the Mark Twain specialist!

The editions are arranged chronologically; at the end are listed those not identified as to date.

1 [Date, 1601.] | Conversation, as it was by the Social Fireside, in | the Time of the Tudors.

DESCRIPTION: Pamphlet, pp. [1]-8, without wrappers or cover, measuring 7x8½ inches. The title is set in caps. and small caps.

The excessively rare first printing, printed in Cleveland, 1880, at the instance of Alexander Gunn, friend of John Hay. Only four copies are believed to have been printed, of which, it is said now, the only known copy is located in the Willard S. Morse collection.

2 Date 1601. Conversation, as it was by the Social Fireside, | in the time of the Tudors.

(Mem.—The following is supposed to be an extract from the | diary of the Pepys of that day, the same being cup-bearer to | Queen Elizabeth. It is supposed that he is of ancient and no- | ble lineage; that he despises these literary *canaille;* that his soul | consumes with wrath to see the Queen stooping to talk with | such; and that the old man feels his nobility defiled by contact | with Shakespeare, etc., and yet he has *got* to stay there till Her | Majesty chooses to dismiss him.)

DESCRIPTION: Title as above, verso blank; pp. [i]-xi, text; verso p. xi blank. About 8x10 inches, printed on handmade linen paper soaked in weak coffee, wrappers. The title is set in caps. and small caps.

COLOPHON: at the foot of p. xi: Done Att | Yᵉ Academie Preffe; | M DCCC LXXX II.

The privately printed West Point edition, the first printing of the text authorized by Mark Twain, of which but fifty copies were printed. The story of this printing is fully told in the Introduction.

3 Conversation As It Was | By The Social Fire-side | In The Time Of The Tudors. | from | Ye Diary of Ye Cup- | bearer to her Maisty | Queen Elizabeth. | [design] | Imprinted by Ye Puritan Press | At Ye Sign of Ye Jolly Virgin | 1601.

DESCRIPTION: 2 blank leaves; p. [i] blank, p. [ii] frontis., p. [iii] title [as above], p. [iv] "Mem.", pp. 1-[25] text, 1 blank leaf. 4¾x6¼ inches, printed in a modern version of the Caxton black letter type, on M.B.M. French handmade paper. The frontispiece, a woodcut by A. E. Curtis, is a portrait of the cup-bearer. Bound in buff-grey boards, buckram back. Cover title reads, in pale red ink, Caxton type, Conversation As It Was By The | Social Fire-side In The Time Of | The Tudors. [The Byway Press, Cincinnati, Ohio, 1901, 120 copies.]

Probably the first published edition. The story of this printing is told by the publisher, William C. Smith of Cincinnati, in a letter to the *American Book Collector,* November, 1933.

"About 1900, there was in existence [in Cincinnati] a small private press called the Byway Press, operated by one Ludlow and Mr. A. E. Curtis. I bought out the Ludlow interest, and having recently come into possession of the 'Fireside Conversation,' I conceived the idea of printing a small edition for private consumption. My copy was typewritten, and in printing the book we followed copy, which fact accounts for the variations in spelling. The edition comprised 200 copies, but owing to the primitive character of the little press, there were a great many copies thrown out because of imperfections, gray printing, etc. The net result was 120 copies."

Mr. Smith, in a recent letter to the writer, states that the type was distributed immediately after printing. Later, in 1916, a facsimile edition of this printing was published in Chicago from plates (see No. 7); and in 1930 a reprint of this facsimile was issued in Chicago (see No. 28).

A Tudor | Coversazione | By ye Social Fireside | in ye 4 Yeare of Our | Lord's Grace | 1601 | [figure]

DESCRIPTION: 1 blank leaf, pp. [i-viii], pp. [1]-[28] text, pp. [xxix-xxxii], 3 blank leaves; 4¾x6⅞ inches; bound in cream colored boards, with dust jacket.

Cover printed in red: In Yᵉ Closet | of Yᵉ Virgin | Queene. | Anno Domini | MDCI. Dust jacket also printed in red. In Ye | Closet Of | Ye Virgin | Queene. | A. D. 1601. |

COLOPHON: Fifty copies printed on Imperial Japan | Vellum in colours throughout, with illum- | inated head-piece and illustratory initial letters in gold and red | and fifty copies on laid paper, in black with head piece and initials in red. | [At bottom of previous page] Swiversdale | 1903:

Illustrated by and printed for George Bentham, a clever Chicago artist, in 1903. Description based upon Vincent Starrett's copy.

5   Conversation | By The Social Fireside | As It Was | In The Time of the Tudors. | Date—1601.

DESCRIPTION: 3 blank leaves; frontis. port. of M. Twain, mounted, Intro. note [i-ii], [1-16] text, 1 blank leaf. 5½x8⅜ inches, Japan vellum, stiff white wrappers. Cover: A Conversazione | in the Year | MDCI. Trefoils all over cover, with black marginal border.

COLOPHON: Printed privately on July the 20th, 1913, in an edition of 75 copies.

Vincent Starrett reports that this edition was printed in Chicago for Guido Bruno.

6   1601. Conversation as it was by the Social Fireside in the Time of the Tudors.

Printed at ye Sign of ye Flea, in ye Citie of Brotherly Love, A. D. 1601. 12 mo., pp. 29, parchment, wrappers, four etchings by Pierre Nuyttens. Printed for the Flatulence Society of Pittsburgh, 1916.
Data taken from Haas.

7   Conversation As It Was | By The Social Fire-side | In The Time Of The | Tudors. | Etc.

DESCRIPTION: Facsimile reprint of No. 3, listed above, except for cover. Same pagination, except that there are no blank leaves fore and aft. 4¾x6 inches, printed on Old Stratford book stock, white paper wrappers, fourfold, white cord tie. Cover reads: A Conversa- | zione | in the Yeare | MDCI, enclosed in a decorative design. Printed in Chicago.

COLOPHON: Printed privately on September the | 28, 1916, in an edition of 500 copies | This is Number . . . |

8   *This Edition of* | *Mark Twain's* | DATE 1601 | CONVERSA-TION | AS IT WAS BY | THE • SOCIAL | FIRESIDE IN THE | TIME OF THE TUDORS. | *Comprising Facsimiles* | *of the Original Edition* | *and the revised or* | *West Point Edition,* | *is limited to* 110 | *copies of which this is* | *No.* —— | *Privately Printed 1920.*

DESCRIPTION: 2 blank leaves, pp. [i-x], pp. [1]-8 [Hay printing]; blank leaf, leaf announcing "West Point" edition, pp. i-xi [West Point printing], 3 blank leaves. 7x9 inches, printed on heavy handmade paper, deckle edges. Title page is completely hand-lettered.

Bound in grey boards, cloth back. Front cover has label "1601" in gilt on black, gilt border. Made in four signatures, [four sheets, fourfold], and stapled.

Frontis. facsimile of autograph note signed "S. L. C." apparently written directly below the colophon in a copy of the West Point edition.

Morse catalogue gives New York as the place of publication.

Mark Twain's | DATE • 1601 | CONVERSATION | AS IT WAS   9
BY | THE • SOCIAL | FIRESIDE IN THE | TIME OF THE TUDORS. |
is limited to 110 *copies of which this is* | No. —— | *Privately Printed 1920*

DESCRIPTION: pp. [1-16] text, 6x9½ inches, brown wrappers, saddle-stitched. Printed on "Bay Path Book" laid paper. Title and cover hand-lettered with same legend as given above for title. Two pages of "Foreword."

Fireside Conversation in the Time of Queen Elizabeth, or   10
1601. A Fragment from Mark Twain.

DESCRIPTION: Privately printed, 1922. 5.2x7.8 inches, boards. Morse catalogue.

Fireside Conversation | in the | Time of Queene Elizabeth | *or* "1601" | [rule] | *A Fragment* | by | MARK TWAIN | [rule] | PRIVATELY PRINTED | 1924

DESCRIPTION: Pp. 16, consisting of title page as above, verso blank; pp.   11
[iii-iv] "Preface", an excerpt from Paine; p. [v] "A Negative Assent",
verso blank; pp. 7-15, text; p. [xvi] blank. 5¼x7⅛ inches, light sand
wrappers, "1601" on front cover. Data supplied by Karl Yost.

1601. Conversation as it was by the Social Fireside in the   12
Time of the Tudors.

Attributed to Fred D. Vanover, Louisville, Ky., 1924. 8vo., pp. 8, wrappers, preface, title page illustration. Limited to 500 copies. Data taken from Haas.

Fireside | *Conversation* | in 1601 at Yᵉ Time of | Queen   13
Elizabeth | By | MARK TWAIN | [cut of Airedale] | Being
Number One of The Airedale Series | Privately Published | 1925

DESCRIPTION: Pp. [i-ii], pp. [1]-18, 2 blank leaves. 5x8 inches, printed on Kinkora laid paper, grey boards, paper label. Cover label: FIRESIDE CONVERSA | TION in yᵉ Goodᵉ Queene | ELIZABETH'S TYME. [Rule border.] Printed in Chicago. Edition limited to 500 copies. Text is preceded by an excerpt from Paine's *Biography,* and a note on the Hay-Gunn correspondence.

14 Fireside Conversation | In The Time of | Queen Elizabeth | 1601 | [printer's device] | Privately Printed.

DESCRIPTION: One blank leaf, pp. [1]-15, one blank leaf. 6¼x9½ inches. Green paper wrappers, red silk tie-cord. Front wrapper has comic pen-and-ink sketch showing Sir Walter exploding at rear, while the other characters stand aghast.

It is reported that this edition was printed in Chicago, 1925.

15 "1601" | OR CONVERSATION AT | THE SOCIAL FIRESIDE AS | IT WAS IN THE TIME OF | THE TUDORS | Privately Printed at San Francisco | Mcmxxv.

DESCRIPTION: 3 blank leaves; Title, verso blank; pp. [iii-x] Foreword by Charles Erskine Scott Wood; p. [xi] half title, verso blank; pp. [xiii-xxix] Text of 1601; p. [xxx] blank; pp. [xxxi-xxxvi] Hay and Gunn letters, etc.; 3 blank leaves. Printed on J. Whatman Hand Made paper, England, 1924, deckle edges. Title in red, rubricated capitals through text. 5x7¾ inches. Printed at the Grabhorn Press. In his Foreword, dated February 20, 1925, Wood says, "At the request of the Grabhorn Brothers I am writing at seventy-three in 1925." On p. [xxvi] is "This present edition of one hundred copies follows it [the West Point edition] word for word and adheres strictly to its orthography and punctuation."

BINDINGS: 25 copies bound in full sheep; 75 copies bound in marbled boards, paper label on backstrip, MARK TWAIN "1601".

16 FACETIA AMERICANA | [rule] | FIRESIDE CONVERSATION | A FRENCH CRISIS | LITTLE WILLIE | THE OLD BACKHOUSE | [rule] | PRIVATELY PRINTED FOR SUBSCRIBERS ONLY. | Nineteen Hundred and Twenty-five.

DESCRIPTION: Pp. [1]-32; printed on Alexandra Japan, 6x9¼ inches, while paper vellum wrappers, front cover, FACETIA | AMERICANA "Fireside Conversation" appears on pp. 5-14.

1601 or, Conversation as it was at the Social Fireside in the 17
Time of the Tudors.

In *Two Worlds,* "A Literary Quarterly Devoted to the Increase of Gaiety of Nations," pp. 118-124, published at the Sign of the Mocki-Grisball, December, 1925, New York City. 500 copies. An expurgated printing which omits three words, two nouns and one verb—"the three most expressive words in the English vocabulary of love."

1601 or, Conversation at the Social Fireside as it was in the 18
Time of the Tudors.

DESCRIPTION: 8vo; 6 leaves; self-cover; 200 copies. Privately printed.

According to Haas this edition is attributed to G. T. Pearson, LaCanada, Calif., 1925. Contains a brief foreword.

Fireside | *Conversation* | in 1601 at Ye Time of | Queen 19
Elizabeth | By MARK TWAIN | [cut of Fox] | Being Number One of the Fox Series | Privately Published | 1926

DESCRIPTION: Pp. [i] half-title, verso blank; pp. [1]-18; 2 blank leaves. 5x8¼ inches, printed on Georgian laid paper, rose colored boards, paper label. Cover label has same printing as No. 13.

Printed in Chicago at the instance of Ralph Fletcher Seymour. Edition limited to 500 copies. Apparently the same plates were used as in printing No. 13, with exceptions as noted on title and six capitals printed in red in this text. Text is preceded by an excerpt from Paine's *Biography,* and a note on the Hay-Gunn correspondence.

Conversation as It Was by the | Social Fire-Side in the 20
Time | of the Tudors | *from* | *Ye diary of ye Cupbearer* | *to Her Majestie* | *Queen Elizabeth* | [device] | Imprinted by Ye Puritan Presse | At Ye Jolly Virgin | 1601.

DESCRIPTION: Pp. [1]-16; title, verso blank; p. [3] Hay's letter, with quote from Saturday Evening Post; p. [4] the "Mem."; pp. 5-16 text. Printed on Bay Path Book laid paper, buff, 5½x6⅞ inches.

Bound in light bistre paper wrappers, with tie cord. On cover: 1601 | [two short rules] | Conversation as It Was by the | Social Fire-Side in the Time | of the Tudors.

According to Ija Adler this edition was printed in Chicago in 1926, in an edition of 200 copies. Data from Karl Yost.

21 Date 1601   Conversation as it was by the Social Fireside in the time of Tudors.

DESCRIPTION: [Montreal, 1926]. Paper wrappers. Morse catalogue.

22 "1601" | OR CONVERSATION AT | THE SOCIAL FIRESIDE AS | IT WAS IN THE TIME OF | THE TUDORS | BY | Mark Twain | Privately Printed | in New York City | MCMXXVII

DESCRIPTION: Two blank leaves; pp. [i-xl]; p. [i] title; p. [ii] limitation; pp. [iii-viii] Foreword; [xii-xxvii] text; [xxix-xl] Aftword; two blank leaves. Printed on Georgian laid paper, 4¼x6½ inches, bound in gorgeously colored boards, orange colored paper back, "1601 | Mark Twain" on backstrip, boxed.

Limited to 125 numbered copies. Earle H. Emmons, typographic designer, has written an entertaining and penetrating Foreword, and in the Aftword has told the story of the Hay and West Point printings with the exchange of letters involved.

COLOPHON: & | Soe, here endeth "1601, or Conversation at the | Social Fireside as it Was in the Time of the | Tudors," as writ by Mark Twain. Desygned & | arranged in typpe by Earl H. Emmons & prynted | on fynne Georgian papers, ye story | itselfe is sette | by hande in ye worshipful Master Frederic W. | Goudy's Italian Olde Style typpes, & ye helle of | a job it was forsoothe, in especial for one whose hande hadde not | touched ye typpe case in up- | wardes of a score of yeeres. The associated matter is machine sette in these same faces, ye style, | ye speling, punctuation & soe forthe following closely ye originalle Weste Pointe Edition donne | in the yeere 1882. Here & there slyghte changes, | for ye sake of ye better spaycing, have beene made, | butte they are soe insignificaunt thatte it was | felt ye results justifide ye meanes and thatte noe one, notte even Mark, | himselfe, wolde object. | Nieu Yorke City, 1927.

23 1601. Conversation as it was by the Social Fireside in the Time of the Tudors.

According to Haas one thousand copies were privately printed in 1928. Reprints the letters exchanged between Hay and Gunn.

24 1601 | OR | A FIRESIDE CONVERSATION | IN YE TIME OF | QUEENE ELIZABETH | BY | MARK TWAIN | [vignette] | *Privately Printed | 1929*

DESCRIPTION: One blank leaf, p. [i-vii] half-title and note; p. [viii]

frontispiece; p. [1] title page as above, p. [3] limitation note; pp. 5-28 text and explanatory material; two blank leaves. 4¾x7½ inches, binding of greenish gray boards, blue cloth back. Front cover reads, in rectangular box, Sixteen | hundred | and one | Twain. The frontispiece and three illustrations are colored. The explanatory matter aft quotes Hay's letter to Gunn, and Twain's letter to Orr. Limited to 40 copies, San Francisco. Description supplied by Karl Yost.

1601 [in red] | *or* SOCIALL FIRESIDE CONVERSATION | IN YE   25
TIME OF YE TUDORS | By MARK TWAIN | [rule in red] |
Being a Curious Extract from ye Diary | of ye Cupbearer
to HER MAJESTY, | Queene Elizabeth, of blessed memory. |
[rule in red] | [three squares composed of printer's devices] | [rule in red] | LOUISVILLE | Printed at *Ye Blew Grasse Press* | Anno. 1929 |

DESCRIPTION: Pp. [i-iv], p. [iii] frontis., p. [iv] title, pp. [i & vi] blank; pp. 1-14, p. [xv] colophon, verso blank. Printed on Linweave Hand Made laid paper, deckle edges, 6x8¼ inches. Bound in boards, light powder blue, with cover title: 1601 | By Mark Twain. The numerals are one and a half inches tall; the letters, in capitals, are 5/16 inches high. Plain white paper dust jacket.

Fireside Conversation in the | Time of Queen Elizabeth | 26
or | "1601" | A FRAGMENT | by MARK TWAIN | [device] |
PRIVATELY PRINTED | 1929.

DESCRIPTION: Pp. [i-v]; pp. 6-30; one blank leaf. Pp. [v]-9; excerpt from Paine's *Biography*; pp. [10]-12, A Negative Assent; pp. [11]-30, text. Printed on Utopian laid paper, 4⅞x6⅝ inches. Light blue wrappers, white silk cord tie. Cover title: Fireside Conversation in the | Time of Queen Elizabeth | *or* | "1601".

Conversation as it was by the Social Fireside in the Time   27
of the Tudors, from ye Diary of ye Cup-bearer to Her
Majesty, Queen Elizabeth.

DESCRIPTION: Pp. 16, 8vo, wrappers. Privately printed [P. Port, 1929] in an edition of 300 copies. Contains a foreword reprinting the letter by John Hay referring to the printing of *1601* and a brief note of introduction. Data taken from Haas. Morse catalogue gives date as 1929.

28 Conversation As It Was | By The Social Fire-side | In The Time Of The | Tudors. | Etc.

> DESCRIPTION: Reprint of No. 7, listed above, from the same plates. 4½x5¼ inches, heavy buff paper, orange paper wrappers, red wool tie. Printed in Chicago in 1930 by John Hecht.
> COLOPHON: This edition of Mark Twain's celebrated | classic, entitled A Conversation in the | Time of the Tudors, is privately print- | ed at The Attic Press & is strictly limited to only five hundred numbered copies | Number

29 "1601", or, Conversation at the Social Fireside As it was in the Time of the Tudors. By Mark Twain. Privately printed by a Hell of a Printer, 1930.

> DESCRIPTION: 16mo., stiff wrappers. Note supplied by Yost.

30 1601. Conversation as it was by the Social Fireside in the Time of the Tudors.

> DESCRIPTION: Pp. 9; quarto, wrappers; 200 copies privately printed in 1931. Data taken from Haas.

31 Fireside | Conversation | in 1601 at the Time of | Queen Elizabeth | *By* | MARK TWAIN | [printer's device] | 1932.

> DESCRIPTION: Pp. 16; 1 blank leaf; p. [i] title; pp. [1]-3, Excerpt from Paine's *Biography,* also a Negative Assent; pp. [5]-13, text; 1 blank leaf. 7x10 inches, tinted laid paper, buff wrappers. [limited to one thousand copies, printed in Chicago for Simon P. Magee] Cover: Fireside | Conversation | in the Time of | Queen Elizabeth | [Printer's device] | A Fragment | By MARK TWAIN.

32 "1601" and Sketches Old and New, New York, The Golden Hind Press, 1933.

> DESCRIPTION: Pp. 204; 6¼x9½ inches. Contains as title indicates the "Sketches."

33 "1601" | OR CONVERSATION AT THE | SOCIAL FIRESIDE AS IT WAS | IN THE TIME OF THE TUDORS | By Mark Twain | With Notes on Mark Twain's "1601" | and a Check-list of Various Editions | and Reprints Compiled by Irvin Haas | [design] | The Black Cat Press • Chicago | mcmxxxvi.

DESCRIPTION: One blank leaf; pp. [i-viii], comprising half-title, frontis., title; pp. 9-16, Introduction; pp. 19-30, text; pp. 33-39, Check-list of editions.

Printer's Note: 300 copies of this volume have been printed | direct from hand-set Caslon type on Worthy | Coronet paper by Norman W. Forgue, who designed and set the type, assisted by Norman | Johnson at the case. The woodcut frontispiece and title page decoration by Ben Albert Benson | are printed from the original wood blocks | Completed at Chicago, March, 1936. This is the first edition to print a check-list of the various editions and reprints.

'1601' | A Tudor Fireside Conversation | As Written by the   **34** Ingenuous, Virtuous | and learned Mark Twain, wit. | [Vignette] | Embellished by the worthy Alan Odle | At London | Printed for Subscribers only and are to be sold at ye beare Back-Side in Maiden Lane | MCMXXXVI.

The title page is printed in black on a yellow panel, as is the text and other illustrations. Quarto, black cloth with gilt stamping.

DESCRIPTION: 1 blank leaf, pp. [i-viii] comprising a fore illus., frontis., title, and page of text, the "Mem.", pp. 1-25, pp. [xxvi-xxix] comprising the last page of text, illus. colophon, and illus., 2 blank leaves.

COLOPHON: This edition of Mark Twain's '1601' | A Tudor Fireside Conversation | has been illustrated by Alan Odle and | has been limited to nine hundred and | fifty copies of which six hundred and seventy copies are for America and | two hundred and eighty copies are for | England. This particular copy being | number | [illustration] | MDCI.

Mark Twain's | 1601 | CONVERSATION | AS IT WAS . . | . . . BY   **35** THE | SOCIAL FIRESIDE | IN THE TIME OF | • THE TUDORS • | [device].

DESCRIPTION: N. p., n. d.; Verso of title reads: Limited to 101 Copies | of which this is No.—— | Privately Printed | London | 1937. Pp. [i-iv); pp. 5-10 Foreword; pp. 11-[29] text; [xxx-xxxii] blank. Printed on tinted laid paper, 4⅞x7¼ inches. Bound in greenish mottled wrappers, printed with same legend as title, omitting the device. Printed in brown ink, each page enclosed in double rule borders.

"1601" | [Fleuron in red] | Mark Twain.   **36**

DESCRIPTION: 32 pages, set in 12 point Bradley, printed on B.R. laid paper, 4⅛x6¼ inches. Covers: black buckram, 1601 | (fleuron). Forematter comprises Introduction by the printer, Edward Martin Moore, The Pony Barn Press, Warrenville, Illinois, 1939.

37 *Mark Twain's* | DATE • 1601 | CONVERSATION | AS IT WAS BY | THE SOCIAL FIRESIDE IN THE | TIME OF THE TUDORS. | *is limited to* 110 *copies of which this is* | No._____ | *Privately Printed.*

DESCRIPTION: Pp. [1-16]; 5⅞x9¼ inches; printed on laid paper. Bound in grey wrappers, fourfold, silk cord tie. Contains a brief forward. Cover printed same as title, except for limitation.
Although similar to No. 9, this edition must not be confused with it.

38 Date 1601. Conversation as it was by the Social Fireside in the Time of the Tudors.

DESCRIPTION: Pp. 16, 8vo, wrappers. Privately printed. Full page illustration and 20 small illustrations. Privately printed, n.p., n.d. Data taken from Haas.

39 An Essay on | Wind | With Curious Anecdotes of | Eminent Peteurs, Etc. [n.p.n.d.]

DESCRIPTION: Pp. 112; 5½x8¾ inches; cloth. "1601" is included as the last sketch in the volume, illustrated with a full page woodcut. Title reads: Fireside Conversation | in the time | of | Queen Elizabeth | 1601.

40 Conversation As it Was By the Social Fireside in the Time of the Tudors (ornament) [Date, 1601.]

DESCRIPTION: Edition of 100 copies, [Charlotte, N.C.], 4.7x6.3 inches, paper wrappers. Data taken from the Willard S. Morse catalogue.

41 A Social Fireside Conversation in the Time of the Tudors. M.T.

DSCRIPTION: 5.7x8.5 inches, paper wrappers. Morse catalogue.

42 [Date, 1601.] Conversation as it was by the Social Fireside, in the Time of the Tudors.

DESCRIPTION: Broadside, 8.5x8.9 inches. Morse catalogue.

43 Conversation, as it was by the Social Fireside, in Ye Time of Ye Tudors.

DESCRIPTION: 8.0x10.0 inches, paper wrappers. Morse catalogue.

44 A Social Fireside Conversation in the Time of the Tudors.

DESCRIPTION: 4.5x5.5 inches, bound in leather. Morse catalogue.